PUFFIN BOOKS

RETURN TO OZ

Many readers may have heard something about Dorothy Gale's first adventure in the marvellous land of Oz, with her good friends, the Scarecrow, the Tin Woodman and the Cowardly Lion. After that first adventure, Dorothy paid many more visits to Oz, and met lots more strange and wonderful characters.

This new Oz story is all about Dorothy's latest exciting visit to that magical country. The Emerald City of Oz has changed: Dorothy discovers that some terrible things have happened since her last visit. The King of Oz, Dorothy's friend the Scarecrow, has been overthrown by the wicked Nome King. The city of Oz lies in ruins, and all its good people have been turned to stone. The cruel Princess Mombi is now living in the Emerald Palace. Dorothy knows she must rescue her friends and restore the city of Oz to its former emerald glory – and with a little help from some friends, that's exactly what she does!

This delightful, magical adventure, based on the Walt Disney film *Return to Oz* (which in turn is based on the original classic Oz stories by L. Frank Baum), has been especially written for Puffin with younger readers in mind.

Alistair Hedley

# RETURN TO OZ

From the photoplay by
Walter Murch and Gill Dennis

Based on the books of
L. Frank Baum

*Illustrated by Jo Worth*

PUFFIN BOOKS

Puffin Books, Penguin Books Ltd, Harmondsworth, Middlesex, England
Viking Penguin Inc., 40 West 23rd Street, New York, New York 10010, U.S.A.
Penguin Books Australia Ltd, Ringwood, Victoria, Australia
Penguin Books Canada Ltd, 2801 John Street, Markham, Ontario, Canada L3R 1B4
Penguin Books (N.Z.) Ltd, 182–190 Wairau Road, Auckland 10, New Zealand

First published 1985

Made and printed in Great Britain by
Richard Clay (The Chaucer Press) Ltd,
Bungay, Suffolk
Filmset in 12/16 Monophoto Palatino by
Northumberland Press Ltd, Gateshead,
Tyne and Wear

# RETURN TO OZ

THE LAND

OOGABOO

SKEEZERS

GILLIKIN

River

N
W        E
S

Old Mombi's

Castle of
The Tin
Woodman

Wicked
Witch   Jack
Pumpkinhead

River

WINKIE
COUNTRY

Scarecrow's
Tower

LAKE

River

Flutterbudget
Rigmarole

Tottenhots

Horners

Utensia

Winkie

Bunbury
Bunnybury

Hoppers

The
Truth
Pond

Hammerhead

YIPS

MOUNTAINS

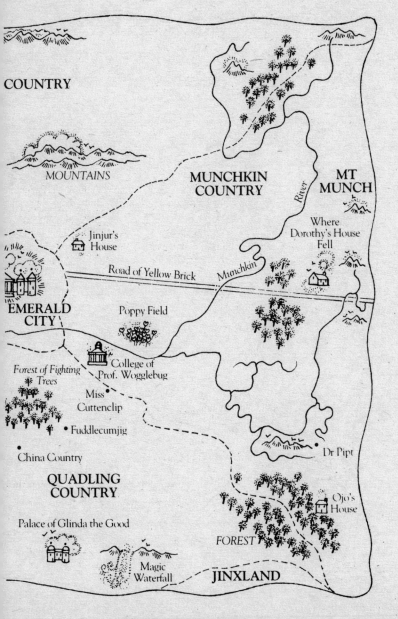

OF OZ ·

COUNTRY

MOUNTAINS

MUNCHKIN
COUNTRY

MT
MUNCH

River

Jinjur's
House

Where
Dorothy's House
Fell

Road of Yellow Brick

Munchkin

EMERALD
CITY

Poppy Field

College of
Prof. Wogglebug

Forest of Fighting
Trees

Miss
Cuttenclip

Fuddlecumjig

China Country

Dr Pipt

QUADLING
COUNTRY

Ojo's
House

Palace of Glinda the Good

FOREST

Magic
Waterfall

JINXLAND

# CHAPTER
# 1

Dorothy was nine, and she lived in Kansas with her Aunt Em and Uncle Henry. They lived in a farmhouse on the prairie, and Uncle Henry worked the hard, baked land and Aunt Em worked with him. They were good people, but they didn't have much time for fun and laughter, and they didn't have much time for Dorothy.

When the great wind came and blew away their house, it blew the spirit out of them. Uncle Henry just sat for long stretches, looking at the ground. Aunt Em grew gaunt and lined and worn with worry. It didn't help that Dorothy went missing with the house, and when she was found swore she had been having adventures in the magical land of Oz.

Aunt Em didn't know what to do. She told Uncle Henry, 'That child is ill. She must have had a knock on the head, or a fit, or a brainstorm. I don't know. She can't sleep for thinking of this blamed land of Oz she's imagined. You ask her to wash the dishes and she tells you instead some fairy tale about a cowardly lion, and a tin woodman, and a scarecrow who rules an emerald city. It's driving me plain crazy too, just listening to her. It's so real to her, poor thing, realer than our troubles, in this half-built house on this bare land. Even that yellow hen Billina has stopped laying. I've told her, "Billina, I want an egg from you, or you're for the pot," but she just sits and squawks.'

'Now, Em, don't get agitated,' said Uncle Henry. 'The hen will lay in God's good time. I'll set to and finish this new house before the winter comes. And the girl will get better, you'll see. Why, this man Dr Worley is advertising in the paper again for his miracle cure: ELECTRICAL HEALING – FOR BRAIN-FEVER, NERVES AND POVERTY OF BLOOD. We could take Dorothy to him.'

'Well, Henry, I don't know, I'm sure. I've meant well by that girl, but I just can't manage her. This Dr Worley's not a regular doctor, so I hear tell, but maybe he can help.'

'It's worth a try, Em,' said Uncle Henry. 'It's worth a try.'

When Dorothy came down that morning, she went straight into the yard to see if Billina had laid. She looked everywhere for an egg. 'Oh, Billina,' she said. 'You're just not trying. You'll end up in a stew if you don't watch out. Aunt Em said so.'

Billina made a nervous scratch at the ground. She seemed to have found something. 'What have you got there, Billina?'

said Dorothy. 'Why, it's a rusty old key!' Dorothy picked it up, and felt the O at the key's end. She pressed out the dirt caught in it, and saw there was a metal letter inside it: a Z.

O, Z. Oz!

'Aunt Em! Aunt Em! Come quick! See what I found: it's a key from Oz. A key from Oz. Now you must believe me about the Cowardly Lion, and the Tin Woodman, and the ruby slippers, and everything.'

Aunt Em came out drying her hands on a ragged old towel. 'What is it now, child? More of your nonsense?'

'It's a key from Oz. Billina found it.'

'Give it here.' Aunt Em looked at the key. 'Why, Dorothy, this is nothing more than the key to our old house, the one that was blown away by the tornado. I must have turned it a thousand times.'

'It's not, it's not, it's from Oz. It's proof. Give it to me.'

Aunt Em held the key away. 'Now, Dorothy, remember what I said?'

'Not to talk about Oz.'

'Why?'

'Because it's just in my imagination.' Dorothy's voice was dull and lifeless. No one believed her.

Aunt Em gave her back the key.

That night, Aunt Em told Uncle Henry she was at her wit's end. 'We'll have to try that Dr Worley's miracle cure.' So next morning she took Dorothy on the cart over the rutted track to the nearby town. In every window they passed, a pumpkin lantern grinned at them, to show that Halloween was coming.

Dr Worley's house was big and white: a mansion beside Uncle Henry's little wooden farmhouse. Aunt Em and Dorothy felt quite nervous standing at the door.

Aunt Em rang the bell, and the door was opened by a lady with a starched uniform, and a severe, starched look on her face. She had a badge on her uniform saying HEAD NURSE WILSON. 'Ah, Mrs Blue,' she said. 'The doctor is expecting you. Come this way.' She walked down the corridor ahead of them, and as she walked she made a prickly, whispering sound, *hiss, sss, sss.*

Head Nurse Wilson led them into the doctor's office. Dr Worley was a big man with a beard. He stood up. 'Mrs Blue,' he said. 'Charmed to meet you. Absolutely charmed. And this must be little Dottie.' He reached out to ruffle her hair.

Dorothy stepped back. 'Dorothy,' she said.

'Of course, of course,' said Dr Worley. 'And now, why don't you sit down and tell me *all* about it.'

So Dorothy started from the beginning, and told him all about Oz. When she had finished, he said, 'Ah, this tiger you mention . . .'

'It was a lion. The Cowardly Lion.'

'Yes, yes. Now this cat could talk, you say, like the scarecrow, and the tin man.'

'Yes.'

'And how did you get back from . . .' Dr Worley looked at his notes '. . . Oz?'

'I *told* you. I put on my ruby slippers, clicked the heels three times, and said "Take me home to Aunt Em".'

5

Dr Worley looked into her eyes. 'Dorothy, where are those slippers now?'

'I lost them. They fell off, on the way home.'

There was a silence. Dr Worley fiddled with the big ruby ring on his finger. Dorothy made a brave little noise in her throat that meant she wasn't going to cry.

'Well, Mrs Blue,' said Dr Worley, 'I think you'd best leave little Dorothy with us. She'll be in the best possible hands. We'll soon have her right as rain.'

Aunt Em looked troubled. 'You promise you won't do anything to hurt Dorothy, Doctor?'

Dr Worley's lips smiled. 'Am I made of stone, dear lady? Don't even think such a thing. There is nothing to worry about. And now, if you take your leave, Nurse Wilson will show Dorothy to her room.'

So Aunt Em told Dorothy to be good, and said goodbye, and left her alone in the big white house, and then Head Nurse Wilson took her to a room, and locked her in.

Dorothy sat in the hard wooden chair by the dressing-table in her room, and looked in the mirror. She thought, I'm all alone, and no one cares about me, and no one believes me.

She looked in the mirror again, and there, behind the glass, was a girl's face! A girl with yellow hair, dressed in white. The girl mouthed something — it might have been 'Oz' — and held out her hand. In her hand was a carved pumpkin head. And Dorothy seemed to reach in to the mirror, and take the pumpkin from her.

Dorothy shook herself. There was nothing in the mirror but her own reflection. Perhaps I *am* going mad, she thought. But there on the dressing-table, smiling up at her, was a carved pumpkin head. 'I'm sure you weren't there before,' said Dorothy.

Just then she heard outside the door the hissing step of Head Nurse Wilson.

'Time to see the doctor again, Dorothy,' said the nurse.

She made Dorothy lie on an awful old trolley that squeaked and squealed, and pushed her to the doctor's office. Dorothy was terrified. Dr Worley made her sit on a shabby old horsehair sofa, and then he took out a big watch from his waistcoat pocket. It swung to and fro on its chain, and its *tick, tick, tick* seemed to fill the room. 'Soon you're going to go to sleep,' said the doctor, 'and then my electrical machine will make you better.'

Outside a storm was blowing up and, as the watch swung, the rain began to lash against the window. It seemed to beat down in time to the watch's tick.

Dorothy tried desperately to stay awake. The lumpy sofa

was itchy beneath her knees. She looked past the watch at the stuffed moose head on Dr Worley's wall. She felt very drowsy.

Just then, there was a tremendous thundercrack, and a searing flash of lightning. All the lights went out. As Dr Worley and Head Nurse Wilson blundered about the room, Dorothy felt a soft pressure on her arm. It was the girl from the mirror!

'Follow me,' said the girl. 'We've got to get you out of here. Dr Worley doesn't heal people. He just uses them for his experiments!'

Hand in hand, the two girls ran from the big white house. Behind them, they could hear Dr Worley shouting, 'Catch her, catch her. She mustn't get away.'

In the dark the two girls slipped down the bank and into the river, turned by the storm from a muddy creek to a

raging torrent. They were swept helplessly along, clinging to a chicken coop that had been carried away from some farmyard on the flood. Soon Dr Worley and Head Nurse Wilson were left far behind.

The next thing Dorothy knew, it was morning. Her friend with the yellow hair was gone. Dorothy was still on the chicken coop: but last night's flood had dwindled to a little pond. From inside the coop, Dorothy heard the cackle of a hen. 'I know that voice,' she said, and she looked into the coop. 'Why, Billina, it's you!'

'So, you're awake are you?' said the hen. 'About time too.'

'Billina! You're talking!'

'Ten out of ten for observation,' said Billina.

'But Billina, if you're talking, then this ... this must be Oz!'

# CHAPTER
# 2

A hot sun was beating down. The pool was shrinking, shrinking till the chicken coop rested on fine dry sand.

'So this is Oz, eh?' said Billina.

'It must be,' said Dorothy.

'Isn't it – if you'll pardon my mentioning it – a trifle ... *sandy?*'

Sand stretched before them as far as the eye could see. Sand, sand, nothing but sand and rock.

'This must be the Deadly Desert,' said Dorothy. 'Be careful. Anything that touches the sand of the Deadly Desert turns to sand itself. I think I can cross by leaping from stone to stone. You'd better fly.'

'Fly?' said Billina. 'Fly? You can carry me.'

So Dorothy tucked Billina under her arm and began to jump from rock to rock. Each time she slipped or teetered, Billina let out a squawk: now was not the time for words. But somehow she got across without falling, and reached the end of the Deadly Desert. She was so happy: too happy to look behind her, and see in every rock on which she had stepped a pair of eyes; the shadow of a face.

Deep in the caverns and rocky places beneath the land of Oz, the great Nome King, ruler of Oz, heard reports of these intruders to his realm. His voice was like gravel, or the grinding of rocks. 'So,' he said, 'she has returned. Foolish girl: foolish, foolish girl. Well, she will keep us amused, she and that tatty bundle of feathers she carries with her. Let her go to her precious Emerald City: Mombi will give her the welcome she deserves.'

'We're safe, now,' said Dorothy. 'Safe.'

Billina poked her head out from under her wing.

'Come on,' said Dorothy. 'Let's go to the Emerald City and see the Scarecrow.'

'Who's he, when he's at home?' said Billina.

'He's the King of Oz, Billina,' said Dorothy.

The earth quaked, as the Nome King laughed.

'King or no king,' said Billina, 'I'm starved. I can't move till I've had something to eat.'

'That's no problem now,' said Dorothy. 'We'll find a food tree.'

'Fruit!' said Billina in disgust.

'Oh, no,' said Dorothy. 'Lunch!'

Dorothy led Billina to a Lunch Tree. Every leaf was a paper napkin. From every branch hung a lunch box, and in every box was

> a ham sandwich
> a pickle
> a hunk of fresh cheese
> a slice of chocolate cake
> and an apple

all nicely wrapped in wax paper.

'Leading you across that desert has given me quite an appetite,' said Billina.

Soon they were fed, and on their way.

'Look!' said Dorothy. 'There's an old derelict building. It's surprising the Scarecrow allows a broken-down old ruin like that to stand. Let's go and look.'

As they looked, Dorothy had the queerest feeling. There was something she knew, but it wasn't words in her mind yet. And then she understood. *'Billina!* This is our house. The house that was blown away. The house that took me to Oz before. But it's all ruined. And where are all my friends? Something's wrong.'

Dorothy stepped back, and tripped over something. It was a brick. A yellow brick. And now, everywhere she looked, she saw bricks, torn from the ground and thrown every which way.

'Oh, Billina,' she said unhappily. 'It's the Yellow Brick Road to the Emerald City. Something *is* wrong. Follow me.'

Dorothy started scrambling along the path of the Yellow Brick Road. She stumbled and turned her ankle almost every step, because the bricks were all askew. But she kept on going, and Billina followed her.

At last, Dorothy and Billina came to the edge of the Emerald City. Its jewelled towers were famous in song; its thoroughfares full of bustle and commotion; its leisured halls of music and entertainment.

The city was desolate. The towers were bare of their jewels. The streets were empty of people. The halls were silent save for the sound of dust sifting down, and the pitter of spiders weaving their webs.

On a pock-marked, ravaged wall, Dorothy could just read the scrawled words BEWARE THE WHEELERS.

'What's a Wheeler?' asked Billina.

Dorothy shook her head. 'I don't know. Something bad, I guess.'

They went on through the ruined city. Everywhere there were statues.

'What a lot of statues there are,' said Billina. 'Look at that funny one, of a man with an axe.'

Dorothy gasped. 'Billina, these are not statues. They're people, turned to stone. That's my friend the Tin Woodman. And look: there's the Cowardly Lion. These are all the people of Oz.'

'What about *them*?' asked Billina, pointing with her wing.

Dorothy looked. There were six young women, dancing in a circle. They were turned to stone, like all the rest. But that was not the terrible thing. The terrible thing was: they had no heads.

The next thing was a noise. Squeal, silence. Squeal,

silence. Squeal, silence. It got louder and nearer. Squeal, silence. Squeal, silence.

There was nowhere to run.

Round the corner came a creature like a man: but it was bent on all fours, and instead of hands and feet it just had wheels. It slithered across the ground, and as it rolled it made that horrible sound. Squeal, silence. Squeal, silence. Squeal.

It spoke. 'Come here, my little chickabiddies,' it said.

Dorothy picked up Billina and ran. And as she ran, she

could hear the Wheeler pursuing her, and the squeal of others joining the chase.

Dorothy ran down a narrow alley, and the Wheelers followed. Squeal, squeal, squeal. The alley ended in a wall. There was a door in the wall, but it was locked. They were trapped.

The first Wheeler squealed to a halt. 'Well,' he said. 'Here's two pretty little chickens. Tender little delicacies for the Nome King.' And he licked his lips.

'The Nome King?' said Dorothy. 'Who's the Nome King?'

'The Nome King, my little morsel, is the new ruler of Oz.' The Wheeler turned to his fellows. 'Three cheers for the Nome King! Long may his stones hold sway!

'Hip Hip —'

'Hurray!'

'But what about the Scarecrow?' asked Dorothy.

And the Wheelers just laughed, and chanted,

> 'The Scarecrow, the Scarecrow,
> Who cares about the Scarecrow?
> We'll pull out all his stuffing
> And we'll dunk it in the po!'

Dorothy's fist clenched in her pocket. How *dare* they be so rude about her friend! And as her fingers closed, they gripped something cold and metallic. It was the key, the key from Oz.

Quick as anything Dorothy had turned, and pushed the key in the lock of the door. It turned, the door swung open, and Dorothy nipped inside, Billina with her.

The Wheelers howled with rage.

Dorothy and Billina were safe. For the moment.

# CHAPTER
## 3

Slowly the clamour outside died down. Dorothy and Billina were left to their thoughts.

'What are we going to do?' asked Billina.

Dorothy made no reply. She just looked helplessly round the dark dingy room in which they had imprisoned themselves. And then she screamed.

There was somebody else in there. A man, standing absolutely still. A little, round man.

Billina gave a frantic squawk.

Still the man did nothing, said nothing.

Dorothy plucked up her courage, and walked towards him. 'Friend, or foe?' she asked. As she walked, her eyes adjusted to the room's dim light. 'Why,' she said. 'It's not a man at all. It's all made of copper. And look, there's something written on its chest.' Dorothy peered. 'ROYAL ... ARMY ... OF ... OZ.'

Dorothy walked round the back of the burnished copper man. There were three separate keys in his back. Underneath

one it said THOUGHT; underneath another, SPEECH; and under the last, ACTION.

'Shall I wind them?' she asked.

Billina was still trying to smoothe her ruffled feathers. 'After a fright like that?' she said. 'Why, it turned my stomach upside down. Leave it alone. What do we want with an old copper kettle?'

'Don't be rude, Billina. He's a soldier of Oz,' said Dorothy.

'I'm going to wind the keys.' She began to turn the key marked THOUGHT. As she did so, she could hear Billina muttering under her breath, 'Copper kettle, copper kettle,' but Dorothy ignored her.

Slowly, the copper man began to tick.

Nothing else happened. 'See what I mean?' said Billina. 'Useless junk.'

Dorothy wound up the key marked SPEECH, and a second ticking joined the first.

'Thank you,' said a new voice.

Dorothy jumped.

'Don't be fright-ened,' said the voice. It was a jerky, mechanical sort of voice, punctuated every now and then by a little wheeze or a swallow between syllables. 'I am Tik-Tok, the Royal Army of Oz. His Ma-jesty the Scare-crow sent me here to wait for Do-rothy Gale. But she has not come.'

'I'm Dorothy Gale,' said Dorothy. 'And this is Billina.' Billina daintily lifted a wing in greeting. 'Tell me, Tik-Tok, what's going on? Where is the Scarecrow? Who is the Nome King?'

'I don't know,' said the copper man. 'When e-very-body began to turn to stone, the Scare-crow sent me here to wait for you. When you did not come, I called for help un-til my voice ran down. Then I paced the floor un-til my action ran down. And then I stood and thought un-til my thought ran down. That is all I know.'

'Why weren't you turned to stone?' asked Billina.

'Be-cause I am not a-live, and ne-ver will be, thank good-ness. It is mes-sy and in-con-ven-i-ent, be-ing a-live.'

'And dangerous,' said Billina. 'What are we going to do about those Wheelers?'

'Wind up my act-ion,' said Tik-Tok,' and I will deal with them.'

So Dorothy wound up the key marked ACTION, and this time Billina kept quiet about copper kettles and junkyards.

When Tik-Tok was fully wound, Dorothy opened the door. Outside were just two Wheelers, curled in the dust and snoring like dogs.

Tik-Tok picked them both up by the scruff of their necks and banged their heads together. 'Asleep on du-ty?' he said. 'That will ne-ver do.' And he banged their heads together again.

The Wheelers squealed with pain and shock, and when Tik-Tok let go, they skidded off as fast as they could go. Billina gave a cackle, and flew up to perch on Tik-Tok's helmet. 'Do it again!' she said.

'I may have to,' said Tik-Tok. 'But I hope not. Let's go.'

Dorothy, Billina and Tik-Tok began to make their way

out of the ruined city. As Tik-Tok saw each familiar landmark defaced or destroyed, he shook his copper head. 'It's lucky I am on-ly a ma-chine,' he said.

At that moment they heard once more the threatening squeak of approaching Wheelers. Round the corner they poured, Wheeler after Wheeler, led by the one who had first chased Dorothy and Billina.

Dorothy held tight to Billina, and Tik-Tok whirled into action. The Wheelers span and swerved to avoid him, but they couldn't. Tik-Tok was tremendous. It was a rout. They fled before him. All but their leader, who stayed flat on his back, his wheels spinning uselessly.

Tik-Tok dragged the Wheeler to his knees. The Wheeler was trembling and shaking. 'You'll be sorry for this,' he blustered. 'Obstructing officers of the Nome King. When he hears how you've treated me, he'll be that angry. I'm his favourite, I am.'

'What is sor-ry?' asked Tik-Tok. 'I am on-ly a ma-chine.'

'What's happened to the Emerald City?' asked Dorothy. 'And who is this Nome King?'

The Wheeler just gulped, as if he had forgotten how to breathe. Tik-Tok picked him up as a terrier does a rat, and shook him till his teeth rattled like hailstones on a windowpane.

'The Nome K-k-k-king is the n-n-new ruler of Oz,' said the Wheeler. 'He c-conquered the Emerald City and took away all the emeralds, and turned everyone to stone.'

'But what about the Scarecrow?' said Dorothy.

'G-g-gone,' said the Wheeler.

'Where?'

'You'd have to ask Princess M-m-m-m-m-m-mombi that.'

'Princess Mombi?'

'She used to be just plain Mombi. She helped the Nome King conquer Oz, and he made her a princess and gave her the Emerald City, once he'd taken the emeralds.'

'What does she look like?'

The Wheeler gave a sly look. 'That's just it,' he sniggered. 'What does she look like? You won't know that till you meet her, and you won't be sure even then.'

'Well,' said Dorothy, 'meet her is what we intend to do. Take us to her.' And they followed the Wheeler through the deserted streets, Tik-Tok holding him by his coat-tails like a dog on a lead. At last they came to Mombi's palace.

'This is it,' said the Wheeler. 'Can I go now? I've brought you to Mombi. That's my part of the bargain.'

'What bargain, buster?' said Billina.

'Yes, you can go,' said Dorothy.

'And don't come squeaking around us again,' said Tik-Tok.

24

The Wheeler rolled away, laughing, a horrid high mocking laugh that sent shivers down Dorothy's back. But nevertheless she knocked at the door and, when no one answered, swung it open, and stepped into Mombi's lair.

As they walked through the corridors and rooms of the palace, Dorothy, Billina and Tik-Tok could hear music drifting by, soft and graceful. They followed it, through the palace, up the stairs, and into the strangest room yet. It was entirely panelled with mirrors. The ceiling was all mirrors, and the floor of polished silver was as good as a mirror. And in every surface, they saw the same reflection: a beautiful young woman, sitting in a chair, stroking a melody from a mandolin.

'Mombi,' breathed Dorothy.

They stepped into the room and, as they did so, a mirrored door slid to behind them.

The woman paid them no attention, but continued to

fondle notes from her mandolin. From her wrist hung a curious key, carved from a blood-red ruby.

'Excuse me,' said Dorothy, 'but are you Princess Mombi?'

The young woman put down her mandolin. She appeared to be studying her face in the wall of mirrors. She patted a loose strand of hair into place, with a lazy, pampered movement.

'I am quite fatigued with playing,' said the young woman. 'It is the emotion. I am so sensitive, and my heart is not strong. Help me to rise.'

Dorothy ran to help her, and the young woman gripped her arm to haul herself out of the chair. She was as strong as an ox.

'I am Princess Mombi,' she said. 'I rule this city. You can serve me.'

'No!' said Dorothy.

'No? The impudence! I suppose you're a princess yourself?'

'Better than that!' said Dorothy. 'I'm from Kansas.'

# CHAPTER
# 4

'Kansas,' said Princess Mombi. 'You're from Kansas. Really. Well, I must put on something more appropriate to welcome you. Your friends can wait here. You come and help me choose.' Mombi renewed her grip on Dorothy's arm, and though it looked to Tik-Tok and Billina as if the Princess were leaning for support on Dorothy, really she was propelling her through the door, which opened before her and closed again after her.

The Princess took Dorothy through her bedroom, with its wonderful crystal bed, into her dressing-room. It was empty save for thirty-one glass-doored cabinets, each elegantly carved from rare woods and marked with a number in gold. Cabinet 25 was empty. Behind the glass door of every other was – the head of a beautiful girl!

'Now what is most suitable?' asked Princess Mombi. 'I always think black looks well on me. Yes, it shall be number 4.' She put her hand to her head, and lifted it from her neck. Then she put it in cabinet 25, and walked across to cabinet 4, which she unlocked with the ruby key round her wrist.

The new head had a mass of black hair, dark eyes, and a lovely pearl and white complexion. As Mombi held it, it spoke. 'What do you think?'

Dorothy gulped. 'I think it is very beautiful,' she said.

Mombi fitted the new head to her smooth neck, then examined herself in the door of cabinet 31, which Dorothy

saw was a mirror and not plain glass after all. 'Yes,' she said. 'Very fetching.'

Then she strode, very fast, one, two, three paces to where Dorothy stood, and gripped Dorothy's cheek tight between fingers and thumb, turning her face this way and that in close perusal.

'Good bones,' said Mombi. 'You have good bones. You will never, of course, be a beauty. Men will not throw their hearts at your feet as they do at mine. But something could be made of you. Your face is not classic, but it has ... character. It could be made really quite attractive. I believe I'll lock you in the tower for a few years until your head is ready, and then I'll take it.'

'You will not!' said Dorothy.

'And who's to stop me, child?' asked Mombi sweetly. 'That bag of rags you call a hen, or that pompous piece of scrap metal that calls itself the Royal Army of Oz? No, *Dorothy Gale*, nothing can save you. I know you and all about you.'

'You don't. You don't,' said Dorothy. 'You don't know me at all. The Scarecrow will save me.'

'The Scarecrow. Much good your precious Scarecrow can do you. The Nome King took him back to the mountains with the emeralds, when he turned all your other friends to stone, save that metal monstrosity in my room of mirrors.'

Dorothy's face brightened at the mention of Tik-Tok.

'So, you still think your copper companion can help you. Come and see.' And Princess Mombi dragged Dorothy back to the mirrored room.

'Tik-Tok! Billina! Help!' she cried.

Billina flew up in a rage and flung herself at the Princess's face: but Mombi plucked her out of the air with a laugh. 'I'll have you in a casserole,' she hissed.

'Tik-Tok! Save us!' shouted Dorothy and Billina.

But though Tik-Tok tried to move, he could not work his copper legs.

'My action has run down,' he said.

He had to stand and watch as Mombi disappeared through the mirrored door with her two captives. He could just hear her answer to Dorothy's despairing cry, 'What will become of Tik-Tok?'

'I'll leave him out in the yard to rust,' said Princess Mombi.

'And I'll leave *you* in here,' said the Princess, as she thrust Dorothy and Billina into a musty junk room, 'until hunger or remorse has put you in a more accommodating temper.'

Princess Mombi barred the door and walked away.

The room had once been grand, but now dust lay thick everywhere, and it looked as though all the furniture that had come to the end of its useful life had just been piled in there to rot.

Dorothy walked over to the high windows at the end of the room. Thick curtains draped to the floor, covered in cobwebs and dust, and full of rents where the old material had decayed. Dorothy brushed them aside, and rubbed a clean patch on the window. She could see below the ruins of the Emerald City, once so proud and handsome. In the distance, beyond the Deadly Desert, loomed the Black Mountain stronghold of the Nome King.

Dorothy felt utterly defeated. She wiped a tear from the corner of her eye. She felt Billina watching her. 'I've got some cobweb in my eye,' she said.

Dorothy turned to look at the room. On one wall hung a faded picture, battered and askew. In it, she could just discern her three old friends: the Scarecrow, the Tin Woodman and the Cowardly Lion. She felt her heart would burst with weeping.

But just then, in the moment before she gave in completely, a voice said, 'Could you just check my head for signs of damage, if it's not too much trouble?'

Dorothy looked around the room. Who could be speaking? Not that moth-eaten old stuffed head of an animal like an elk. Not the sofa. Not the Royal Palm in the corner. Certainly not Billina.

And then Dorothy saw, against the wall, a jumble of sticks of different lengths and thicknesses that might, just might, have once been a makeshift sort of body. And among the sticks was a pumpkin, with round eyes carved in it, and a triangular nose, and a great gaping grinning zigzag of a mouth, that made you smile just to see it.

'Talking vegetables now,' said Billina, who was in a very cross mood.

'Manners, Billina,' said Dorothy. 'Good morning, sir. I'm Dorothy Gale, from Kansas, and this is Billina.'

'From Kansas, too,' said Billina, 'and I wish I was back there.'

'I'm Jack Pumpkinhead,' said the pumpkin head, 'and the atmosphere in this room is doing me no good, no good at all. Please look in my head for signs of spoiling, and put my limbs back together.'

'Of course,' said Dorothy. 'But how did you get in this dreadful state?'

'Mombi threw me down here. She said she was going to bake me in a pie. But I think she's forgotten all about me.'

'Who *is* Mombi?' asked Dorothy.

'Mombi is a witch, and my mother, who made me, was her slave. Mombi brought me to life with a magic powder she bought from a magician, just to see if it worked. And then she magicked my mother away, and threw me in here.

So you can see, I've not done much in the world yet. And this damp is torture to my head. You're sure there are no brown spots?'

'You're a lovely healthy orange,' said Dorothy, 'and you're all jointed up again too. Do stop fussing, and tell me more about this magic powder.'

'The Powder of Life?'

'Yes.'

'Well, you sprinkle it on something, say the magic words, and the thing comes to life.'

'Is there any left?'

'There's bound to be. Mombi keeps it in cabinet 31, the one you can't see inside.'

'Then I've got an idea,' said Dorothy. 'We'll fly out of this prison, and go to the Black Mountain and rescue the Scarecrow.'

'I hope you don't think I can carry you all,' said Billina. 'I can hardly carry myself.'

'No,' said Dorothy. 'We'll make a flying creature: with those two old sofas for a body, and palm leaves for wings, and that funny head for a head. What animal is it, anyway?'

'That?' said Jack Pumpkinhead. 'That's a Gump.'

'Well, whatever it is, it will do. The first thing is to get out of here, and fetch Tik-Tok from the room of mirrors.'

'That's easy,' said Jack Pumpkinhead, and he stood up, his joints cracking. 'Oh, my poor knees and elbows,' he said. Then, flexing his twiggy fingers, he went to the door. There was a grille in the door through which the Princess could gloat over her captives. Jack put his long thin fingers through the grille, and under the bar. He lifted it, and they were free.

They went directly to the room of mirrors, where they found Tik-Tok standing motionless just where they had left him.

'Tik-Tok, this is Jack Pumpkinhead,' whispered Dorothy,

as she wound up Tik-Tok's action. 'Jack, this is Tik-Tok, the Royal Army of Oz.'

'En-chan-ted I'm sure,' said Tik-Tok.

'Don't you find these mirrors give you a terrible head-ache?' said Jack.

'Go upstairs, the three of you, and get to work on that Gump,' said Dorothy. 'I'm going to fetch the Powder of Life.'

And Dorothy stole ever so quietly and all on her own into the bedroom of Princess Mombi.

# CHAPTER
# 5

Princess Mombi was huddled beneath the blankets on her crystal bed. Only one arm lay outside the covers: and from the wrist of the arm dangled – so inviting, so terrifying – the ruby key.

Dorothy crept up to her, and held her own breath as she watched Mombi's blankets rise and fall, rise and fall, rise and fall, with the steadiness that only comes with sleep. Dorothy gently took hold of the key, and began to ease its black ribbon over Mombi's hand. It came oh so gradually over the faultless skin. Then, when the key was almost off, Mombi turned over in her sleep, pulling her hand away. What a *cheat*, thought Dorothy. But then she saw, like a gift on the bedspread, the blood-red ruby key nestling in its velvet ribbon.

Dorothy took the key into Mombi's dressing-room, trying not to look at the sinister heads in the cabinets. She went straight to number 31. She recoiled: there was a head here, too. But then she realized it was only her own face,

pale in the door's mirror. She turned the key, to see what she would see.

The head inside cabinet 31 was hideous: with hair like snakes and horrid yellow-lidded eyes. But while Mombi slept, it slept too. It was Mombi's original head, and it was guarding Mombi's most precious spells and potions. And of all these precious charms, the most precious of all was the one marked POWDER OF LIFE.

Dorothy reached out and took the box of powder. But as she withdrew her hand, she knocked a bottle of evil-looking liquid. It fell, and smashed, and the head, the deadly head, awoke.

The yellow lids raised, and saw the thief. The snake-like locks hissed, *sss, sss,* and struck at her. And the bodiless mouth yelled, 'DOROTHY GAAAAAAA-LLLLLLLLE!'

Dorothy turned and ran, back into the princess's bedroom. Mombi was awake, and sitting up in bed. She had no head. And then Dorothy realized that every cabinet had been full. There were no gaps. And without a head, Mombi could not see.

Dorothy darted back into the dressing-room, shut the door on Mombi's monstrous head, and locked it with the ruby key. And then she walked slowly through Mombi's bedroom, easily avoiding the groping headless figure which sought to trap her.

Dorothy went into the mirrored room. She looked at all the reflected Dorothys on every surface. Which one hid the mirrored door? In her panic, she couldn't tell. The muffled wailing of Mombi's thirty-one locked-up heads was driving every sensible thought out of Dorothy's mind.

But as she looked, Dorothy caught a glimpse of something behind one of the Dorothy-images. A blurred something, like a shimmer of smoke, like the shape of a person, almost like another girl. But then it was gone. Dorothy went to that reflection, and pushed, and the door opened. Then Dorothy ran up the stairs, and back to Billina, Tik-Tok, Jack Pumpkinhead and the Gump.

The Gump was nearly finished, but the wings weren't on. Billina and Jack were looking very strange, and Tik-Tok was talking nonsense: all slurred and peculiar, a mixed-up jumble of words and grinding sounds.

'Tik-Tok's gone mad,' said Billina.

'Nonsense,' said Dorothy. 'His brains are just a bit slack, that's all.'

'How dreadful to have a brain that ticks down,' said Jack.

'It's more common than you think,' said Dorothy, as she wound up Tik-Tok's THOUGHT key. 'Now come on, Jack, Billina, Tik-Tok: there's not a moment to lose. Tie on those wings.'

Dorothy opened the box of magic powder, and sprinkled it on the now-complete Gump.

Nothing happened.

'What's wrong?' asked Dorothy. 'Why isn't it alive?'

'You've got to say the magic words,' said Jack.

'What are they?'

'I don't know.'

40

The four friends looked at each other. Was it all for nothing? Downstairs they heard the sound of breaking glass, as Mombi smashed her way into cabinet 31 and picked out her own exquisitely horrible head. She was coming. If she caught them this time, there would be no escape.

'Such an undignified end, to finish up in a pie,' said Jack Pumpkinhead in a worried tone.

'Look in the box. Look in the box,' squawked Billina.

And, sure enough, inside the lid of the box there were instructions.

The friends clambered on the Gump, and Dorothy pronounced the magic words:

'Weaugh – Teaugh – Peaugh!'

The Gump began to twitch.

Mombi appeared at the door, like a vindictive black bat.

'Come on, Gump!' the friends shouted.

The Gump began to beat his wings. And as he beat faster and faster, a great gust of air blew out the windows, and the Gump took off, and the friends cleared the windowsill inches ahead of the witch, who could only yell curses after them.

It was the Gump's first flight, and for a first attempt it wasn't bad. But the way the Gump dived uncontrollably, then straightened up, then flew straight at a wall, or a tree, then wandered in an unplanned circle, kept the friends' hearts in their mouths.

The Gump spoke first.

'What's going on?' it said. 'The last thing I remember is being in the forest, then hearing a loud bang. I seem to be flying. I couldn't do that before. And something's happened to my body. This one I've got now feels as if it might fall apart at any moment.'

'Oh no, Gump, don't let it do that!' cried Dorothy. 'You've got to carry us to the Nome King's mountain, to rescue the Scarecrow.'

'I'll try,' said the Gump. 'But I warn you, I'm not very well made.'

And at that moment, there was a twang of snapped rope, and one of the Gump's wings sagged aside.

'Don't worry,' shouted Jack, 'I'll hold it on.' Jack reached for the broken rope and held it, leaning over the edge of the two sofas that were lashed together as the Gump's body.

From there, Jack could see the ground spreading out behind them. And he could see, on that ground, the Wheelers, in hot pursuit.

'We're being followed,' he shouted. 'Quicker, Gump, quicker!'

The Gump put on a burst of speed that surprised even

himself, and soon the friends were flying out over the Deadly Desert, with the Wheelers still frantically following, baying inhumanly.

The Wheelers were so intent upon the Gump up in the sky, they never noticed when the firm earth turned to deadly sand. They skidded and screeched as they tried to halt, but each and every one spilled on to the Deadly Desert, and turned to sand, so that now the fearsome Wheelers are just shifting grains in the desert dunes, at the mercy of every wilful breeze.

The friends flew on, across the desert – where Dorothy dropped Mombi's ruby key – and to the other side.

Everything was going well, till Jack let out a wail.

'My *headdddddddd* ...' he called.

And when the others looked, sure enough, Jack's body ended in a simple spike, and his pumpkin head was plummeting to the earth.

The Gump turned round and went into a dive. Soon they were level with the falling head, and Dorothy was stretching out to grasp it. But it was just outside her reach. 'Can you hear me, Jack?' she shouted.

'I ... feel ... very ... dizzy,' he replied.

'We'll have to get un-der you,' said Tik-Tok, 'or in-stead of a pump-kin, you'll just be a squash.'

Dorothy reached out even further: too far. She

43

overbalanced, and would have fallen, had not Jack's body reached out and grabbed her. As it did so, it let go of the rope it was holding, and the Gump fell apart.

'Abandon ship!' shouted Billina. 'Hens and children first!'

And then they were all falling, falling, falling, to a cliff edge.

One of the sofas landed first. On top of the sofa landed Dorothy, winded but unhurt. And on top of Dorothy landed Billina, for all the world like a feather duster without a handle. Next to them landed Jack's body, and on top of that, fair and square on the spike of its neck, landed Jack's head.

On the very edge of the cliff landed Tik-Tok, one hand valiantly clutching the Gump's antlers. Also attached to the Gump's antlers was the other sofa, and this, slowly but surely, was pulling the Gump and Tik-Tok over the cliff.

Jack caught hold of one arm, and Dorothy took the other, and they tried to haul Tik-Tok up. But the sofa was too heavy for them. Billina fluttered down, and pecked at the rope securing the sofa to the Gump. Strand by strand, the rope gave way, and as it clattered down the cliff, Tik-Tok and the Gump catapulted to safety.

'That was a close-run thing,' said Tik-Tok.

'Yes,' said Jack, 'but what a queer place this is we've landed in. Everything's upside down.'

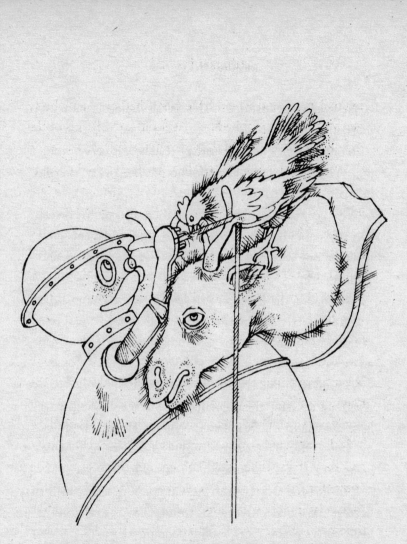

'Only your head, silly,' said Dorothy. 'Here, let me put it on properly.' She lifted off Jack's head. It had suffered no damage, barring a hole smashed in the removable lid, caused by landing the wrong way on the spike.

Jack was not pleased. 'This is all I need, with my migraines,' he said.

'Nonsense, Jack,' said Dorothy. 'That hole is very becoming. Why, it's just the latest fashion in headwear, isn't it, Billina?'

'Yes, very chic,' said Billina. And then she said to herself, 'I've had enough of this. I'm for some peace and quiet.' And while no one was looking, she crept inside Jack's head, and went to sleep.

Meanwhile the friends were seeing to the Gump, who was a sorry creature indeed: just a stuffed head and a trail of frayed rope. Still, as the Gump himself put it, 'It's been an experience.'

'A head with-out a body's no good,' said Tik-Tok. 'I vote we give the Gump the re-main-ing so-fa. It's got legs, so at least the Gump will be able to get about. He may waddle a bit, but that can't be helped. There's worse things than wadd-ling.' Tik-Tok himself had a rather rolling gait.

'Oh no you don't,' said the Gump. 'I'm a Gump: the fleetest, most graceful of all the forest animals. I can't move like a sofa! What if I met another Gump?'

'You won't meet another Gump,' replied Dorothy. 'That's a very good idea, Tik-Tok.' So they lashed the Gump's head to the sofa with the end of the rope.

'Now we're ready for the Nome King,' said Dorothy.

# CHAPTER
## 6

'Ready for me, are they?' rumbled the Nome King. 'We shall see. *We shall see.* That fool Mombi – Princess, indeed! – has let them get away, though at least she seems to have got rid of that hen. But though they escape Mombi, and her charade of changing heads, and though they turn my pretty Wheelers to dust, and though they cross the Deadly Desert unharmed, they shall not escape me. I have been wronged too much by these creatures who crawl on the earth's surface and rive my rocks in their greed for jewels and minerals. They shall not escape.'

In the room of mirrors in her castle, Mombi, too, plotted revenge. 'I will go to the Nome King,' she told herself. 'He will give me justice. My ruby key stolen; my Powder of Life wasted on a stuffed Gump's head and a pair of horsehair sofas. It is not to be borne!' She picked up her mandolin, and strummed it idly. As she plucked the strings, she ventured nearer and nearer to the note at which glass shatters. She lingered round that note, teased at it, but she never struck it. And every sound she made was an unspeakable agony to the smoky indistinct spirit trapped in the mirrored door. Watching her prisoner writhe, Mombi was filled with a bitter, savage glee. 'That's right, little one,' she crooned. 'That's right. Dance, dance. It's all you can do. No one is going to save you. No one knows where you are.' Mombi cackled. 'There's not anybody left who even remembers who you are. Think about that, while I am away.' With that, Mombi put down her mandolin, and descended into the depths of her castle, to the secret tunnel that would take her safe to the Nome King's mountain.

On the cliff top, the friends celebrated their lucky escape. The Gump was still keeping a wary eye out for other Gumps, so he could take cover before he was seen, but he was secretly feeling rather pleased with his new body. Being a horsehair sofa, it was remembering the sun on its coat, and frisky days in the meadow, and despite its squat little wooden legs, it was trotting along with a jaunty rhythm. Jack Pumpkinhead, too, was feeling quite pleased with himself, and the fashionable new cut of his head. Billina, who was snug inside that head, was chuckling contentedly to herself. Tik-Tok was fully wound-up. And Dorothy was humming herself a little tune.

So none of them was ready for the voice that came to them out of the very rocks at their feet, a voice like the

beginning of an avalanche, that said, 'Stop!'

The voice had the icy politeness of a stone dropped in a pool. It sent ripples of unease through Dorothy.

It said, 'Tell me who you are, and why you are trespassing in my kingdom, and what I can do for you.'

'It's the Nome King,' whispered Tik-Tok.

'If you please, Your Majesty,' said Dorothy, 'I'm Dorothy

Gale, and these are my friends, Tik-Tok, Jack and the Gump.'
She thought it best not to introduce Billina, in case the hen
forgot her temper in the Royal presence.

'Not *the* Dorothy Gale, from Kansas?' asked the Nome
King.

There was a ripple in the ground, as if the cliff was
laughing. In a rock ahead, Dorothy thought she could make
out the shadow of a face, bearded and rather frightening.
But the voice had mellowed, and Dorothy thought, perhaps
the Nome King's not so black as he's been painted.

'Yes, Your Majesty. I am that Dorothy Gale. I've come
to ask you to release the Scarecrow, and to restore the
Emerald City. It was so beautiful, and now it's all forlorn
and crumbling.'

'You believe I have stolen something, Dorothy, and you
want me to give it back?' asked the patient, understanding
voice. Dorothy was beginning to quite like it, and couldn't
understand what had made her think of avalanches and
threats at first.

'Yes, Your Majesty,' she said.

'If someone steals something, you think the right thing
for them to do is to give it back.'

'Of course,' said Dorothy.

'And if that someone doesn't want to give it back?' asked
the voice.

'Then they should be made to,' said Dorothy.

'By whom?' asked the voice.

'By the honest people,' said Dorothy. 'And by the army.'

'Army?' asked the voice.

Tik-Tok stepped forward. 'Roy-al Ar-my of Oz, stan-ding to atten-tion, sir!' he bellowed, and he clicked his copper heels. 'Show him we can do things prop-er-ly in Oz,' he whispered to Jack.

But the Nome King didn't seem impressed. First he smiled. Then he chuckled. And then he laughed. He laughed fit to burst, and the whole cliff shook with him.

Where Dorothy stood, the ground parted, and she tumbled headlong down, into the depths of the earth: the heart of the Nome King's realm. And as she fell, passing through rock as easily as if it were water, Dorothy experienced in her body the stubborn hopelessness of rock, that holds so grimly to what it contains, yet in the end must yield it up. And she felt behind her eyes the beauty of secret colours on which no light has ever shone; flesh, blood, muscle and bone of her was admitted to the intimate society of the earth's interior.

And then Dorothy was careering across a floor of polished obsidian, in a huge underground cavern, and coming to a stop by a rock face in which she could see, so much more clearly than before, the stern features of the

Nome King. And after passing through the layers of rock, she understood so much better than before what she saw in that face: the grudging, miserly capriciousness of it; its greed, its sorrow, and its cruelty.

The Nome King spoke, in a voice that was firm and calm and infinitely terrifying. 'All the metals in the world, and all the precious stones as well, are made here, in my underground dominions. They belong to me. They are made by the Nomes for my ... amusement. And yet you *insects* from the surface dare to rifle my secret hiding-places, plunder my treasures, and use them as baubles for your preening vanity, and counters in your pitiful games of barter. You squander the riches of the earth, and you expect me to stand idly by. No! No! A thousand times no! I am the Nome King.'

And hundreds of invisible Nomes chanted, 'Three cheers for the Nome King! Long may his rocks hold sway!'

'Hip Hip –'

'Hurray!'

'But you have so much,' said Dorothy. 'Surely you can spare us something. And anyway, that doesn't give you the right to bully people, and imprison the dear Scarecrow. He never took anything of yours, or wanted it either.'

'The Scarecrow is a thief: a rotten thief like all you surface-crawlers.'

'He's not, and I want to see him.'

'By all means, by all means.' The Nome King's voice boomed. 'Bring forth the prisoner.'

And there, across the cavern, bound by invisible tethers and held by invisible warders, was the Scarecrow, with the crown of Oz still sewn to his head.

'Dorothy!' he cried.

'Scarecrow!' she answered.

And that was all they said, and all there was to say.

Then there was a thunderous crack, and a flash like blue lightning, and the Scarecrow disappeared.

'What have you done to him?' asked Dorothy in anguish.

'I have turned him into an ornament: an amusing trinket for my palace. I will keep him for all time, as a punishment for thievery, and as a warning to others.'

'But he never stole the emeralds! They were already there when he arrived! It's not fair.' Dorothy was in a passion of grief.

And the Nome King reached out a stone hand to her. 'Now, now,' he said. 'We mustn't give way. There's no rift without a trace of ore. Don't cry.'

Dorothy could not speak through her sobs. 'The emeralds were ... they ... were ... already ... when he ...'

'No, no, don't cry. Poor, poor Dorothy Gale from Kansas. This is not how a brave little rock behaves.'

'Not ... thief ... not ...'

'Now then, we can't have this. We can't have this. I tell you what, Dorothy. You dry your eyes and blow your nose, and you and I shall play a little game. Your friends can help you, and if you win, you can have the Scarecrow. Now that's worth a little risk, isn't it?'

Dorothy nodded, and swallowed down her sobs, though she couldn't help sniffing. 'That's worth any risk,' she said.

# CHAPTER
## 7

As Dorothy calmed herself, Tik-Tok, Jack and the Gump appeared, propelled by invisible Nomes.

'Just in time!' said the Nome King. 'You're just in time to join Dorothy and me in a little game. I'm sure you're all good at games. Probably far too good for my old granite brains.'

The others looked at Dorothy.

'Let's do what he says,' she said. 'It's the only hope for the Scarecrow. The Nome King has turned him into an ornament.'

'Exactly so, exactly so,' said the Nome King. 'You catch on quick. Now: these are the rules of the game. One by one you can go and inspect my collection of ornaments. Each of you has three chances to guess which ornament is really the Scarecrow. If you touch the right object and say the word "Oz", you will release the Scarecrow from my spell, and you will be free to go. Now, what could be fairer or more fun than that?'

'We accept,' said Dorothy.

'Oh good!' said the Nome King. 'I do enjoy a game. Now: why doesn't the sofa go first.' The rock face behind the Nome King parted like a curtain, revealing a passage behind.

The Gump stayed still.

'Come on, sofa! Look lively!' said the Nome King.

'Gump,' said the Gump. 'I'm a Gump.'

'Look like a sofa to me,' said the Nome King. 'But as you like.'

'I haven't got any arms to touch with,' said the Gump.

'Use your antlers,' said the Nome King.

So the Gump set off on his stumpy wooden legs down

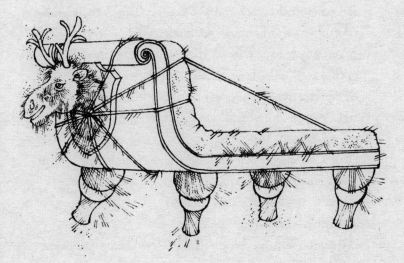

the stone passage, to the cavern where the Nome King kept his ornaments.

The friends listened to the trit-trotting echo fade away. There was a distant peal of thunder.

'I'm forgetting myself,' said the Nome King. 'It's so long since I've played host. You must be tired, and want refreshment. STOOLS!' he bellowed, and instantly stools appeared. They were carved out of huge emeralds. 'Now,' said the Nome King. 'A little something to eat and drink, perhaps? I usually nibble a millstone at this time of day, and take a sip or two of molten silver. Does your fancy turn that way?'

'No – no thank you. Nothing at all, thank you,' said a flustered Dorothy. Jack and Tik-Tok just shook their heads.

There was another peal of thunder.

'Your Ma-je-sty,' said Tik-Tok.

'What is it?' asked the Nome King.

'If we touch the right or-na-ment, we free the Scare-crow. We have won. But what if we touch the wrong one? What hap-pens to us?'

'What happens to you?' asked the Nome King. 'Why, you become part of the game.'

There was a third peal of thunder.

Dorothy went white. 'You mean ...'

'Oh yes,' said the Nome King. 'The Gump is now an

ornament too. A knick-knack. A trinket. A conversation piece.'

'That's not fair,' cried Dorothy. 'It's *not fair*.'

'Fiddlesticks!' said the Nome King. 'It seems fair enough to me. And I make the rules, so I should know. So come on: time for the next contestant.'

'I'll go,' said Jack Pumpkinhead.

'No!' said Dorothy.

'I tell you what,' said the Nome King. 'I'll only count the wrong guesses. You can go on guessing as long as you guess right. How's *that* for fair?'

'It's all right, Dorothy,' said Jack. 'I won't mind being an ornament. It will be hardest on you, because you are used to eating and sleeping, and breathing, and all that kind of caper; I'm not, so I won't miss it. To be an ornament may be an adventure.'

'Don't talk like that!' said Dorothy. 'We won't be ornaments. We won't.'

She hugged Jack's frail body. 'Take care,' she said. She peeked inside Jack's head. 'You too, Billina,' she whispered.

'This pumpkin needs his head examining,' said Billina.

And then they were gone.

Dorothy and Tik-Tok just looked at each other.

They heard the first peal of thunder.

'One guess gone,' said Dorothy.

'I am not even a-live,' said Tik-Tok. 'It will not be so hard for me as for you, Do-roth-y.'

'Oh, Tik-Tok,' said Dorothy.

'Yet I have en-joyed tick-ing,' said Tik-Tok.

They heard the second peal of thunder.

'I do not hold out much hope for Jack,' said Tik-Tok. 'He

is a fine fel-low, but not one of the world's great think-ers.'

'Oh, he's not as empty-headed as he looks,' said Dorothy with a smile.

There was silence.

'Do you need winding?' asked Dorothy.

'My thinking could be tight-er,' replied Tik-Tok.

Dorothy wound up the key marked THOUGHT. 'It's too bad they didn't make you self-winding, Tik-Tok!' She turned her head, so her salt tears did not fall on his burnished metal.

'I am a mere ma-chine,' said Tik-Tok. 'I must accept the faults in my de-sign, and do the best I can.'

They heard the third peal of thunder.

'What fun this is!' said the Nome King. 'Next!'

Tik-Tok patted Dorothy on the shoulder. 'Don't wor-ry, Do-roth-y,' he said. 'I will find a way.'

Tik-Tok went down the passage, and Dorothy was once more all alone with the Nome King.

Two thunderclaps sounded, in quick succession.

When the Nome King spoke, his voice was quiet. But beneath it was a mounting excitement.

'Tell me, Dorothy,' he asked, 'why did you really come here?'

'I told you why.'

'Oh, come now. Your friends are not here. We are alone. No one can hear us. You can tell me.'

'I told you why.'

'You came all this way for a scarecrow?'

'For the Scarecrow.'

'Are you sure it was not for ...' the Nome King raised the hem of his stone robe '... THESE!'

'My ruby slippers!'

'No, Dorothy. *My* ruby slippers. All rubies are mine by right. And these rubies: these rubies are powerful, as you know. They just fell out of the sky one day ... You were so anxious to get home. And they have proved most useful. Most useful. Why, without these ruby slippers, I could never have conquered the Emerald City. Yes, it's all due to you, Dorothy! Thank you. I believe in giving credit where it's due.'

Dorothy was aghast. Her stomach felt like concrete. It was all her fault. If she hadn't carelessly lost the ruby slippers, the Nome King and Mombi could never have ravaged Oz. The thought was like a bitter taste in the back of her throat.

She heard a Nome whispering something to the Nome King. She didn't care what it was. Life was cruel.

The Nome King frowned. 'Dorothy,' he said. 'Your Army has stopped guessing and is standing perfectly still in the middle of the room. Is this some sort of joke?'

'His action must have wound down,' said Dorothy. 'I

wound up his thought, but I must have forgotten to do his action.'

'Well, you'd better go in and wind him up,' said the Nome King. He sounded distinctly annoyed.

Then the Nome King smiled. 'And you can stay in there, and guess for yourself. Unless ...'

'Unless?'

'Unless you'd rather go home.'

'Go home?'

'Yes, home. You don't need to go down there. There's no hope. Forget about them. They're not even human. You've got to look after yourself in this world. I'll let you have the ruby slippers, and you can wish yourself back home, and never think about Oz again.'

# CHAPTER
## 8

'Poor Nome King,' said Dorothy. 'You don't even understand about friends.' And she set off down the dark rock tunnel towards Tik-Tok.

The Nome King remained, looking sadly at the ruby slippers.

There was a commotion in the Nome kingdom. The King could hear a familiar voice, shrill and querulous, demanding, 'Take me to him at once! At once, do you hear! I have urgent news for the Nome King! Let me through, fools!' And into his presence came the owner of the voice, the witch Mombi, wearing her own hideous head with its hissing snake-like locks.

'Kneel,' said the Nome King.

Mombi knelt.

'Lower,' said the Nome King.

Mombi sprawled on the polished floor.

'What brings you to disturb my peace?' asked the Nome King.

'Your Majesty ... the girl ... the girl from Kansas ... *Dorothy Gale* ... she's here, in Oz ... she's come back.'

'I know. You were supposed to deal with her.'

'She stole my ruby key, and my Powder of Life! And valuable antiques which she made into a flying sofa. She's heading this way with ... with ...' Mombi dried up in fear. She had just looked into the Nome King's eyes.

'You're too late, Mombi,' he said, in a deadly, passionless voice. 'You're always too late. You're incompetent. A nincompoop. An out-and-out failure. Go and drown yourself in a bucket of lard.'

'But Majesty ...' Mombi's face was twisted with fear. Saliva was dribbling from the corner of her mouth. 'But Majesty, what about the girl?'

'The girl is safe. She and her *friends* are among my ornaments. She has just three guesses to free them. She will fail. And then I will turn her into something pretty and useless, and keep her for ever and ever. She will never wither and grow old. She will never change. Never.'

'But what if she guesses right?'

'She will not guess right.'

'But if she did? She could find out about Ozma. She could ruin everything.'

'Ozma.' The King savoured the word in his mouth.

'*Ozma.*' Then he glared at Mombi. 'Ozma! You haven't let her escape too, you snivelling gobbet of grease?'

'No, Your Majesty. Of course not, Your Majesty. Ozma is hidden. Ozma cannot escape.'

'Then all is well. The others have failed in their guesses, and so will Dorothy Gale.'

There was a murmuring of thousands of Nome voices: 'Dorothy Gale. Fail. Dorothy Gale. Fail. Dorothy Gale. Fail.'

The murmuring hummed in Dorothy's ears as she ran down the passage to the Nome King's ornament collection. Her very heart seemed to thump out the message: Dorothy Gale, fail.

Tik-Tok was standing motionless in the centre of the ornament cavern. Dorothy ran to wind him up.

'Why, Tik-Tok! You're all wound up! You've not run down at all.'

'I told you I would find a way. Watch me while I choose: see what hap-pens. I have one guess left. If I guess in-cor-rect-ly, you will see what I change in-to.'

'Tik-Tok, you're a genius! That will give me a clue. We'll show the Nome King.' Dorothy threw her arms right round Tik-Tok's round little body. She could feel something wet on his cheek. She touched it with her finger: it was a droplet of oil, warm oil. 'Why, Tik-Tok, what's this?'

'A ma-chine mal-func-tion. That is all.'

And Tik-Tok reached out and touched the nearest object,
and said, 'Oz.'

There was a burst of thunder: a flash of lightning: and
Tik-Tok was gone.

Dorothy looked and looked for something that was not
there before, but she couldn't see anything. Tik-Tok had
vanished without trace, like all the others.

'I don't suppose ornaments *mind* being ornaments,' she
said to herself. She reached out and touched a bowl. 'Oz,'
she said.

Thunder rolled.

She touched a crystal glass, and said 'Oz' again.

Thunder rolled.

Now there was but one more chance, one slender hope. Dorothy closed her eyes and, arms outstretched, walked randomly about.

Her hands brushed against something soft. She reached out to grasp it. She didn't say 'Oz'. Something wasn't right. The thing in her hand was hard. She opened her eyes. She was holding a little brass owl. But next to the owl was a green pincushion.

Dorothy put down the owl, picked up the cushion, and said, 'Oz!'

There was no thunder. There was no flash. Just the Scarecrow, large as life and twice as natural.

'Suffering stalactites!' shouted the Nome King. 'Shiver my striations! The girl has done it!'

But Dorothy didn't know how she'd done it, or how to do it again, and the Scarecrow didn't either.

'I don't even know what I was,' said the Scarecrow.

'You were a green pincushion,' said Dorothy. 'Perhaps all the others will be pincushions, too. Or perhaps they will all be green. Perhaps things from Oz remember the grass and the trees, and turn into green ornaments.'

'That must be it,' said the Scarecrow. 'Let's look for something else green.'

Dorothy and the Scarecrow looked all over the cavern, and at last they found a green ink-well. Dorothy touched it. 'Oz.' And there was the Gump.

'Gump!' cried Dorothy. 'You're safe! Was it dreadful being an ornament?'

'It was, ah ... educational,' said the Gump. 'But I have

to admit, a trifle lacking in variety, a trifle limiting, a trifle cramping. In a word: dull.'

'Let's look for Jack and Billina and Tik-Tok. Look for anything green.'

The three of them continued the search. But as they did so, the whole cavern began to shake. All the ornaments began to topple, and smash. The Scarecrow saved one, a green porcelain fruit basket, just before it hit the floor.

And then, through the floor, with a sound like the world coming to bits, rose the Nome King's head, scattering rock and debris everywhere.

Dorothy ran to touch the fruit basket, and said, 'Oz.' It was Jack, looking very bewildered.

'STOP THIS!' roared the Nome King. 'STOP!'

'But I haven't finished guessing,' said Dorothy. 'You said you wouldn't count correct guesses.'

'I'm tired of that game,' said the Nome King. 'And I'm tired of you. I'm tired of the lot of you.'

The Nome King's huge stone hand burst through the floor. In it, screaming, was the witch Mombi. The Nome King took one pitiless look at her, and stuffed her down his great stone gullet, that was ribbed with layers of rock laid down through all the ages of the world.

The friends listened, horrified, to Mombi's dwindling cries as she plummeted down, down, down to oblivion.

# CHAPTER
## 9

Dorothy, Jack, the Scarecrow and the Gump stood for one dreadful second rooted to the spot as the Nome King swallowed Princess Mombi. Then they fled, through the crumbling ruins of the ornament cavern. Great lumps of rock crashed about them as they ran. The air was thick with choking dust.

But whichever way they ran, there was no way out.

The Nome King approached.

The great stone fingers clenched round Jack Pumpkin-head's ankles. The Nome King's mouth was open wide. He was going to slip Jack down his throat like a heron gobbling a trout.

And then the Nome King froze. For he heard, from Jack's head, the most terrifying of all noises.

'*Kut-kut-kut, ka-daw-kutt!*'

It was Billina.

'A *chicken*,' sighed a thousand Nomes, their voices whistling round the cavern like a breeze.

Then the stem-topped cap of Jack's head fell off, into the Nome King's mouth: and following it — ever so, ever so slowly — toppled AN EGG.

A thousand Nomes cried, *'Death, death, death,'* and were gone.

The Nome King's mouth snapped shut.

'All things must have an end,' he said. He set Jack down tenderly. 'You have defeated me.'

'But how?' said Dorothy. 'I don't understand.'

'Don't you know, child, eggs are poison to such as I? The egg is life, growth, change. That egg is now in my heart. And in the fires of my heart, the egg will develop, quicken into life. The chicken will awake. I feel it stir. It begins to peck, peck, peck at the shell. Strong is the shell, but the chicken is stronger. It will shatter my heart. You have won.'

There was a thunderclap like the first bang that formed the world; a flash like the first light that shone on the world. And then, blackness, silence.

Dorothy stepped forward, as a dim light returned. Where the Nome King had been was a mound of fractured stone. Dorothy let her hand rest, briefly, on it. Then she leant forward and picked out from the rubble something that glinted: her ruby slippers.

The Nome King's world was caving in round them. Dorothy tore off her old shoes, and put on the ruby slippers.

'Take us all back to Oz!' she said, and she clicked her heels.

Then they were standing on a grassy slope outside the ruined Emerald City. Dorothy, the Scarecrow, Jack, Billina and the Gump. 'I command all the emeralds to be returned to the Emerald City, and all those who were turned to stone to be restored to life,' said Dorothy, and clicked her heels again. Instantly, it was so. The Tin Woodman, the Cowardly

Lion, the girls whose heads Mombi had stolen, all the citizens of Oz came to life. The Emerald City glowed with all its old brilliance.

'What a trip!' said Jack. 'It's taken the top of my head off!'

Dorothy laughed. 'Yes! We'll have to get that fixed, or Tik-Tok will never let you hear the last of it.' Then she gasped. 'Tik-Tok! Where is he?'

'We never found him,' said the Scarecrow. 'He lies, brave Army, beneath the fallen stones of the Nome King's realm. All honour to the Royal Army of Oz.'

Dorothy bowed her head. Here was defeat at the heart of victory. The Gump bowed its head, and from its antlers something fell. It was green: a medal of polished copper.

'It's one of Old Stony's ornaments,' said Billina.

Dorothy reached out and touched the medal. She held her breath.

'Go on, Dorothy,' said the Scarecrow.

'Oz,' breathed Dorothy.

And there, standing among them and ticking away furiously, was Tik-Tok.

'Where am I?' said Tik-Tok. 'Where is the Nome King? What is hap-pen-ing?'

'The Nome King is defeated,' shouted Dorothy, 'and Oz is saved!'

'Hur-ray,' said Tik-Tok. 'Hur-ray!'

And he was echoed by countless voices from the Emerald City: 'Hurray, Hurray, Hurray!'

And the conquerors strode down into the Emerald City, on a path of flowers, and on every side there was cheering and rejoicing, because Oz was free, and the Nome King was no more.

In all the celebrations, Billina had the place of honour:

'And quite right too,' she said. But Dorothy and Tik-Tok and Jack and the Gump were carried shoulder high throughout the city, and Jack was given a new top for his head, and the Scarecrow was seated once more on the Royal Throne of Oz.

# CHAPTER
# 10

Everyone gathered for a celebration party in the mirrored room of the castle. The Tin Woodman was there, and the Cowardly Lion, and the Scarecrow on his throne, and Tik-Tok, and Jack Pumpkinhead, and Billina and Dorothy. The Gump was hanging on the wall, after saying that sofas were all very well in their way, but that having a body that wanted to gallop but couldn't was very wearying.

The Scarecrow said, 'I can't thank you all enough. You risked everything to rescue me.'

'Not at all, not at all,' murmured the company.

'I want you to know,' said the Scarecrow, 'that I had a lot of time for thinking when I was a prisoner of the Nome King, before he turned me into an ornament when Dorothy came. Plenty of time to use those brains I longed for. And now I know I am not cut out to be a king. Too many brains is as bad as too few, when you have to make decisions.'

'But who is to rule if you don't?' asked Dorothy.

Everybody looked at her.

'Stay here and rule over us,' said the Scarecrow.

'Me?' said Dorothy.

'Yes!' said the Tin Woodman. 'Be the Queen of Oz!'

'Queen of Oz!' shouted everyone there, with one voice. Dorothy waited till they were quiet.

'You're such kind, dear friends,' she said. 'I wish I could stay. But I must go back to Kansas. Aunt Em and Uncle Henry will be worrying. But I do wish you could have a queen – a real, proper queen, to set everything right.' Absentmindedly, Dorothy clicked her heels.

'Look! In the mirror!' said Billina.

In the mirror there was a form, at first smoky and indistinct, but growing clearer every second. It was a girl: a girl in white silk robes, with yellow hair and a circlet of silver on her brow.

Dorothy walked towards the mirror, and the image came nearer. Every move that Dorothy made, the girl in the mirror made too.

'Why,' said Dorothy, 'it's the girl from Dr Worley's, the girl who saved me.'

Dorothy reached out her hand to the hand of the girl. Their fingers touched, and when they did the glass of the mirror rippled like water, and through it stepped the imprisoned girl.

'Mother,' said Jack Pumpkinhead.

'Who are you?' said Dorothy.

'Ozma, Queen and rightful ruler of Oz,' answered the girl, in a voice as clear and pure as a mountain stream. 'My father, Pastoria, was King of Oz before the Wizard came: but he was bewitched by Mombi, and sold me to her as a slave, in return for a potion of eternal life. He promised her the first living thing that greeted him when he got home, thinking it would be his dog: but it was me. When he realized what he had done, my father threw away the potion, and killed himself. But I grew up as Mombi's slave, and before Mombi imprisoned me in that mirror, I made Jack Pumpkinhead. Now I am free, if you will have me as your queen, Jack will be my first adviser.'

And all the crowd roared, 'Ozma, Queen of Oz!'

Dorothy bent and took off the ruby slippers, and put them on Ozma's feet. 'These are yours,' she said.

Then Dorothy straightened up. 'It's time for me to go,' she said. 'Please, wish me back to Kansas.'

'Yes,' said Ozma. 'But do not feel alone. For every now and then when you look in a mirror, I will be there. We will not forget you.'

'And I won't forget you,' said Dorothy. 'But I won't be alone. I'll have Billina.'

'No, Dorothy,' said Billina.

'You're not ... you're not coming back?'

'No. Go back, to scratch every day in the dirt and end up in the pot? Go back, at the mercy of every animal that likes to snap a neck and taste a juicy mouthful? Go back, and be dumb again? No, Dorothy, I'm not going back.'

The world began to spin.

'Oh, no!' cried Dorothy. 'I'm not ready! I haven't said goodbye properly.'

She heard her friends calling, 'Farewell. Farewell,' and she felt the lightest of touches, it might have been a hen's wing, and she was gone.

'Farewell, Dorothy, Dorothy, Dorothy.' The voices echoed in her ear.

'Dorothy, Dorothy, Dorothy.' Other voices were coming close.

Dorothy was lying in the mud, on a river bank.

'Dorothy! Oh, Dorothy!' Uncle Henry was on his knees

beside her, cradling her head. Aunt Em was wrapping a blanket round her.

'Oh, Dorothy,' said Aunt Em. 'We'd almost lost hope.'

There was a whole party of searchers, haggard, unshaven, bleary-eyed. And they were all smiling, and laughing.

Aunt Em and Uncle Henry took Dorothy home.

They passed the charred ruins of Dr Worley's mansion. Dorothy looked at Aunt Em. 'Was he . . . ?'

'Killed. And good riddance. And that Nurse Wilson. Killed by the lightning catching those infernal machines. Everyone else got out. And do you know, that Worley wasn't a real doctor at all! He was an evil man. The things he did . . . Well, we don't have to think about that now. I just don't know what was going through my head, to leave you in such a place. Well, we won't be parted again.'

The cart turned into the yard, where the hens were scratching for corn. 'We've lost that dratted hen Billina,' said Uncle Henry.

'And now, young lady,' said Aunt Em, 'it's bed for you. You go and get ready, and I'll come and kiss you goodnight.'

Dorothy got changed into her night-things. She knew this time there was no point in telling Aunt Em about Oz. She looked in the pivoted mirror on her dressing-table, to fix her hair, and there, staring back at her, was Ozma, with Billina in her arms!

'Aunt Em! Aunt Em! Come and look!'

'What is it, Dorothy?'

Dorothy saw Ozma put her finger to her lips.

'Oh, nothing, Aunt Em. Just a reflection.'

Dorothy could hear Aunt Em's footsteps. She tilted the mirror towards the ceiling.

'Not in bed yet? Come on, slowcoach. And put that mirror straight, child. It's not for playing.'

Dorothy hesitated, then slowly tipped the mirror back.

Aunt Em looked at her own reflection in the mirror, and at Dorothy's. 'You're looking a bit peaky,' she said. 'We'll have to plump you up.' And she gave Dorothy a big hug.

## DINNER LADIES DON'T COUNT
### *Bernard Ashley*

Two stories set in a school. Jason has to prove he didn't take Donna's birthday cards, and Linds tells a lie about why she can't go on the school outing.

## DRAGONRISE
### *Kathryn Cave*

A very funny story about Tom who finds a friendly dragon under his bed. The only problem is that the dragon wants to eat Tom's sister. Tom couldn't allow this – or could he?

## BRIDGET AND WILLIAM
### *Jane Gardam*

An easy-to-read, highly illustrated book about Bridget's pony William, who proves his worth in a great snow storm: and a story about Susan, who was determined to save the huge white horse, two hundred years old, cut out of the hillside.

## HIGGLETY PIGGLETY POP!

*Maurice Sendak*

Based on the old nursery rhyme, this modern fairy tale tells how Jennie the terrier packs her bag and goes out into the world to look for something more than everything!

## THE FURTHER ADVENTURES OF GOBBOLINO AND THE LITTLE WOODEN HORSE

*Ursula Moray Williams*

Two highly lovable characters meet and go in search of Gobbolino's sister, Sootica, who is apparently being held captive by a wicked witch.

## THE OWL WHO WAS AFRAID OF THE DARK

*Jill Tomlinson*

In this warm and endearing book, Plop the baby barn owl, conquers his fear of the dark with the help of some interesting and unusual people, and a wise, mysterious cat.